The Guru Returns To The Mountain

Antonio Kazan

By Three Methods We May Learn Wisdom:
Reflection which is the Highest
Imitation which is the Easiest
Experience which is the Bitterest
-Confucious

THE GURU RETURNS

Waiting for waiting
The wave to ride
The right one
Not the wrong one
Then comes the waiting of the windy gales
Which I now stand upon...
the great leviathan of life either way prevails

A small cup of rice wine
A great banter of laughter
The broth of soup simmering on the table
Such delight
Overflowing euphoria

一小杯米酒
笑話
桌上的燉湯
這樣的快樂
溢出的欣快感

Waking to feel the heat of the day
Work to be done
Studying to be done
Dark hours of the night done
Daily hours much to do

much of the world to see and show
□Such work though is never in a day won . . .

The tales of many lives I have heard
The wales of many lives I have heard
every word... □Some were my own
Yet I have changed... thus transformed □.
.It can be done... it can be shown
The essence of being is to struggle
□Are you a wizard or be you a muggle
□Yet you can change . . . thus be informed
□Some you will like . . . Some you will not
□The essence of learning is that the mind and
heart have thus performed . . .

Beauty is of humanity
a duty like a white snowflake in the summer
slow and sudden
□until it dissipates into a cluster with other of its kind
□yet always humanity wishes for such things to rewind

□the hunger of such voices
□fast and furious
hearts made of glass
stones made of hurt
enables feelings to be inert coupling
becoming light as a feather
such are the trials of walking under heavy weather
An eroding river of happiness
An evaporation of such
Are desire and kindness too thus much?
The days of pushing boulders on one's shoulders
□must come to the top
□And then when one must stop . . . ?
Beauty is of tranquility a pot of green tea...

美是人
責任就像夏天的雪花
緩慢而突然
□直到它與其他同類消散成一個集群
□然而人類總是希望這樣的事情倒帶
□渴望這個聲音
□速度與激情
玻璃做的心
受傷的石頭
讓它感到懶惰
變得輕如羽毛

這是在惡劣天氣中行走的考驗
侵蝕幸福的河流
這種蒸發
慾望和善良太多了嗎？
搬石頭的日子
必須在頂部
然後當一個人不得不停下來的時候。..?
美麗是一壺寧靜的綠茶……

A Rose in Prose read
Taking the weight from an other's back
Finding happiness in everything
Carrying that weight around on my proverbial back
Shoving it all up my nose..and head expunging
ZEN

Blood and tears
Yet only random thoughts
Random thoughts randomly placed
Eventually the blood dries
Eventually the tear dies
Yet I live
The blades of negativity
Are soft when touching my skin
Yet they still draw blood
Blood can be replenished
Thoughts can be replenished
Random or not....

A day of snow and rain
I cherish my hat
Covering everything but my thoughts ...

一天的雪和雨

我珍惜我的帽子
涵蓋一切，但我的想法...

The grass of home colored green
The foxes to fly through such high grass
My homeland even with clouds overhead much can be seen
The nights are nice cool and sublime
Drowning myself in nature
Not to die but a splash out in a different time

Orchids to a guest
Rose to the best
Daisies for the children
Does giving ever rest?

Spring sails across seasonal sky
The bright sun numbs the gentle cool
The breaking of some twig sounds in my ear

Every note of nature rings to me so dear

Where to travel as I return home
The way of Zen undetermined I only look at the clouds
To hate the unknowing
Is to hate even learning?...

As I walk poems abound
Such is the material when all of the nature is around
Songs of the heart
Hums of the mind
Bon voyage this town
Another awakens at the foot of my sound

What is good?
Faith from the heart;

Wisdom from the mind;
existence from Zen

What makes a man does good?
The way he feels with his heart
The way he thinks with his mind
The way he exists within Zen

What is right? Coexistence of the three
What is wrong? Confusion of the three
What is truth? The Purity of the three

什麼是好的？
發自內心的信念；
頭腦中的智慧；
禪的存在

是什麼使男人做得好？
他內心的感覺
他的思維方式
他在禪宗中的存在方式

什麼是正確的？三者並存
怎麼了？三者的困惑
什麼是真相？三者的純度

Mouse, mouse a big mouse
Our desire but we can't eat

The sun passes three years
Human nature to hoard but yet we are no-mouse..

The servant is goodness
Smooth and charming is the rule
This courtesy-this feature-so beautiful
In all things to humbly be careful
Before a servant is taught only to obey
To exert effort for sake of dignity
The king takes in the meaning
The royalty in name spreads
The universe...

老鼠，一隻大老鼠
我們的願望，但我們不能吃
太陽過去了三年
人性to積，但我們不是老鼠。

僕人是善良
規則和迷人是規則
禮貌-此功能-如此美麗
在所有事情上要謙卑小心
在教僕只服從之前
為了有尊嚴而努力
國王的意思
特許權使用費差價
宇宙。。。

Reflective Philosophy
反思哲學

As one apple corrupts another so does one aspect corrupt another. One must be decisive with the aspects. They must all flow in the same direction and if possible the same velocity. If not there will be a negative result creating a negative feeling, thought and/or existence.

正如一個蘋果腐蝕另一個蘋果，一個方面也腐蝕另一個方面。一個人必須在方面具有決定性。它們必須全部流向相同的方向，如果可能的話，速度相同。如果沒有，就會產生負面的結果，產生負面的感覺、思想和/或存在。

What is harmony? A oneness of the aspects
What is time? Human knowledge of existence and the passage of action.

什麼是和諧？方面的統一性
時間是什麼？人類存在的知識和行動的通道。

Time affects only the mind and heart. The spirit has an immaterial sense of time. The spirit is the link to zen but that is not to say the other aspects are not as important but one can say with the spirit that it is closer in proximity to it.

時間只影響頭腦和心靈。精神有一種非物質的時間感。精神是禪的紐帶，但並不是說其他方面不那麼重要，而是可以說與精神更接近。

The nexus or focus of placement is a point-between the physical world and the metaphysical one. This point cannot be seen and is not the same for everyone. If one can concentrate on this point one can be will become enlightened. Physical abstracts(money, body, food) spiritual abstracts (magics, sorcery, necromancy) deter one from this point. One is said to be at or close to this point at birth and thus slowly drift away as one gets older. This is due to the aspects and abstracts.

Physical time: Human concept
Spiritual time: Time outside the human conceptual

The further one drifts from the aspects the easier it is for the abstracts to intervene and take over. There is a rhythmic process when the aspects are aligned which results in a creation of energy which can be positive or negative. The same is said for the abstracts. There is the left and the right; the yes and the no, the up and the down.

放置的連接或焦點是物理世界和形而上學世界之間的一個點。這是無形的，也不是每個人都一樣。如果一個人能專注於此，一個人就會開悟。物理抽象（金錢，身體，食物）精神抽象（魔法，巫術，死靈術）阻止一個人這樣做。據說一個人在出生時處於或接近這一點，因此隨著年齡的增長而消失。這是由於方面和摘要。

物理時間：人類概念

精神時間：超越人類概念的時間

離這些越遠，摘要就越容易乾預和接管。當階段對齊時，會有一個有節奏的過程導致能量的產生，這可以是積極的或消極的。摘要也是如此。有左右；是或否，上下。

The Three Aspects:
Heart the nucleus of emotion
Though the nucleus of thought
Spirit – the nucleus of Zen

- Reflective philosophy -

As one apple corrupts another, so does one aspect corrupt another. So a person must be one with their aspects. They must flow in the same direction and if possible even the same speed. If not, a negative backlash may result, which in turn will create a negative action, feeling or existence.

What is Harmony? - A oneness of the aspects
What is time? Human knowledge of experience and passage of action

Time affects only the mind and heart. The spirit version of time is immaterial. The spirit is the link to the what one may call the soul and to further regions of the universe.

The nexus or focus of placement is a point between the physical world and the spiritual world. This point cannot beseem and need not beseem. This point is to some called Zen, The holy spirit or even enlightens. Physical abstracts(money; sex; power etc.), Spiritual abstracts (magic; sorcery; witchcraft etc.) can deter one away from this point. Yet it is possible that the opposite may happen. One is said to be at this point at birth speaking of the nexus and the n as one gets older, one drifts away due to this abstract and yet even others. It can be said that the point of adulthood is to get back to the point of the Nexus.

Physical time: The human concept of time
Spiritual time: Time outside the physical world of existence (physical 6*7*8) is said to be the estimate of this time.

三個方面：
心是情感的核心

雖然思想的核心
精神——禪的核心
- 反思哲學 -

正如一個蘋果腐蝕另一個蘋果，一個方面也腐蝕另一個方面。所以一個人必須與他們的方面是一體的。它們必須以相同的方向流動，如果可能，甚至必須以相同的速度流動。否則，可能會導致負面的反彈，進而產生負面的行為、感覺或存在。

什麼是和諧？- 方面的統一性
時間是什麼？人類關於經驗和行動的知識
時間只影響頭腦和心靈。時間的精神版本是無關緊要的。精神是與人們所謂的靈魂以及宇宙其他區域的聯繫。

放置的聯繫或焦點是物理世界和精神世界之間的一個點。這一點不能被認為也不需要被認為。這一點對一些人來說就是禪宗，聖靈甚至啟蒙。物理抽象（金錢；性；權力等），精神抽象（魔法；巫術；巫術等）可以阻止一個人遠離這一點。然而，相反的情況也有可能發生。據說一個人在出生時就談到了關係，隨著年齡的增長，一個人由於這個抽象甚至其他人而逐漸消失。可以說，成年的意義在於回到連結點。
物理時間：人類的時間概念
精神時間：存在的物理世界之外的時間（物理6＊7＊8）據說是這個時間的估計。

The further the aspects are not unison with one another, the easier it is for the abstracts to bring them apart even further. Regardless the path to bring together is always a narrow path. There is a rhythmic process when the process of the creation of energy is present. It forces out energy which can be positive or negative. This effect produces negativity or positively of an action, feeling or existence. This in turn depends on one's position with one's aspects and the allowance of the abstracts. When one strays from the center of one's aspects there will be an eventual event or events that either shock one back to the center or even take them further away.

這些方面越不一致，摘要就越容易將它們進一步分開。無論如何，走到一起的路總是窄的。當能量產生過程發生時，就會有一個有節奏的過程。它迫使能量可以是積極的或消極的。這種影響會產生消極或積極的行動、感覺或臨在。這又取決於一個人的立場，以及對摘要的許可程度。當一個人偏離自己的靈態中心時，最終會發生一個或多個事件，要么將人震回中心，要么甚至將他們拉得更遠。

What is life? The time on the physical plane in which memories will transcend after sometime into other planes and other aspects of your lives.

What is death? The time when one is so distant from one's aspects that the physical part of them does not exist any more it is also the time the physical apparitions that corrupt the aspects don't exist either.

Keeping the three aspects in focus keeps one in tune with Zen. Keeping the three aspects distant from themselves will create a disturbance n one or both areas. The distance is subjective and it's what is between them that also matter.

The answer to an answer is a question.
The response to forgiveness is acknowledgment
The response to insight is guidance

生活是什麼？在物質層面上的時間，記憶會在一段時間後超越其他層面和你生活的其他方面。
什麼是死亡？當一個人與一個人的某些方面相距甚遠，以至於他們的身體部分不再存在時，也是當破壞這些方面的物理幽靈也不存在時。
專注於禪的所有三個方面。讓這三個方面遠離自己會分散其中一個或兩個方面的注意力。距離是主觀的，它們之間的距離也很重要。
一個答案的答案就是一個問題。
對寬恕的回應是承認
對洞察力的回應就是指導

 As stated there are three aspects of human life. The heart which is the engine of emotions both positive and negative. The mind which is the house of emotions and the spirit or as some would call it the Essence of essentially whom you are in the other planes of existence is the state of an emotion. Emotions and actions create energies. These energies in turn create waves. Both can be deemed positive or negative.

如前所述，人類生活涉及三個方面。積極情緒和消極情緒的引擎。作為情感和精神之屋的大腦，或者像某些人所說的那樣，本質上是你在其他存在層面上所處的人的本質是一種情感的狀態。

情緒和行動創造能量。這些能量反過來會產生波浪。兩者都可以被認為是積極的或消極的。

What is thought? The creation of a response through a situation. What is ingenuity? A thought created by situation that is spontaneously brought on by experience or instinct.

What is intelligence? The amount of accumulated knowledge of this world or others as well as facts and opinions that one knows. What is wisdom? The process of the deliberation and usage of said intelligence.

What is love? The complete focus or incomplete focuses of one's attentions and affections. This can be certain to the abstracts and aspects. As there are many aspects and abstracts, there as many types of loves as well.

什麼是思想？根據上下文創建響應。

什麼是巧思？從經驗或本能中自發產生的情境思維。

什麼是智能？關於這個世界或其他世界的累積知識量以及一個人所知道的事實和觀點。

什麼是智慧？審查和使用上述情報的過程。

什麼是愛？一個人的注意力和感受的完全或不完全集中。這可以被識別為摘要和方面。因為有很多方面和總結，所以愛的種類也很多。

One strives to learn for what reasons? And what is reason? Reasoning is the conceptual theory of analyzing facts and opinions to produce a consequential effect. There are two main types. Dynamic reasoning creates the desired effect quickly and quietly and without hesitation. This type of reasoning is usually used in an on the spot reactive situation. Whereas static reasoning is a reasoning of contemplation. It could be said that Zen perhaps a third type is a combination of the two. One must realize that each of one's aspects has it's one reasoning capability per se. If all reason is collected into one area by the aspects, this is called equilibrium. The effect obtained from this spans quickly to the other regions related to reasoning. This reasoning makes one's time of contemplation immaterial because the desired effect is learned and gained without noticing.

一個人努力學習的理由是什麼？是什麼原因？推理是一種概念理論，它分析事實和觀點以產生相應的效果。有兩種主要類型。動態推理迅速、安靜、毫不猶豫地創造出預期的效果。這種推理通常用於現場反應情況。而靜態推理是一種沉思推理。可以說，禪也許是第三種，兩者的結合。必須認識到，每個方面本身都具有推理能力。如果所有的原因都被這些方面歸為一個領域，這就是平衡。由此產生的影響迅速跨越到與推理相關的

其他領域。這種推理使一個人的沉思時間變得無關緊要，因為所需的效果是在沒有註意到的情況下學習和獲得

What is existence? The factors of perpetual being in a point in time and space but as one knows there is both a spiritual and physical existence present.

 Physical existence-. This where you are now. The material body and world as you know it. This body of yours is constantly bombarded with factors which plague ad poison the physical aspects. The abstracts must be avoided but if they can be avoided, they must me minimized. Therefore, if one's aspects are in line in unison, this can be ample protection against the abstracts. As in most cases the unison of all three is of course difficult, so in that case there must be one aspect that can be the most stable in any or most situations. This is called the stability theory of existence. You see the aspects are the foundation of your existence. Build upon your strongest aspect and the others may fall in line or at the most if a shock-wave should occur you will be ready and prepared.

什麼是存在？永恆存在的因素在時間和空間的一個點上，但眾所周知，存在精神和物質存在。

物理存在-。這就是你現在所在的地方。你所知道的物質身體和世界。你的這具身體不斷受到各種因素的轟炸，這些因素會影響身體方面的

因素。摘要必須避免，但如果可以避免，我必須盡量減少它們。因此，如果一個人的方面是一致的，這可以充分防止摘要。在大多數情況下，這三者的統一當然是困難的，所以在這種情況下，必須有一個方面在任何或大多數情況下都是最穩定的。這被稱為存在的穩定性理論。你看到這些方面是你存在的基礎。建立在你最強大的方面，其他方面可能會順勢而為，或者最多如果發生衝擊波，你就會做好準備。

There are Six levels of existence based on age hereby outlined. There are said to be other levels but I have discovered six to be the foundation.

Level 1 Birth – One naturally at the Existence of Zen at this time
Level 2 Post Birth- ages 1-3 years. At this point awakens one to the abstracts but one cannot comprehend them fully

Level 3 Adolescence – 4 -12 years. This is where essentially the abstracts start coming into play. Especially the physical abstracts. It is at this point. One strays from Zen are quite noticeable.
Level 4 Teenage 13-19 years.

Level 5 Post teenage year's 20-30 years / A most influential time in one's life. This is the midway of existence. It is here, but the abstracts are extremely bombarding the aspects

Level 6 Descending years 30+. At this time if there hasn't been a shock-wave of existence one or more, one is sure to follow. It is at this time where one's reasoning, intelligence as well as wisdom accumulated will make or break a person.

這裡概述了六個基於年齡的存在級別。據說還有其他層，但我發現六個是基礎。

1級誕生——此時自然有禪意存在

等級 2 出生後 1-3 年。在這一點上喚醒一個人，但沒有完全理解他們的總結

3 年級青春期 - 4-12 歲。這就是摘要發揮作用的地方。尤其是物理文摘。正是在這一點上。與禪的背離是相當明顯的。

4 級 13-19 歲的青少年。

5 級 20-30 歲的青少年後/最有影響力的人生時期。這是存在的一半。它就在這裡，但摘要被這些方面轟炸了

6年級降序30歲以上。這個時候，如果沒有一個或多個衝擊波存在，它肯定會隨之而來。正是在

這個時候，一個人的推理、智慧和積累的智慧將決定一個人的成敗。

What are contrasts? They are basically opposite reactions according to the abstracts and aspects. For example, one may experience the abstract lust. Its contrast could be the aspect of love but it may also but it's correspond. This is not the only reaction but it is merely an example. The motion of anger contrasts with calmness. Sadness contrasts with happiness. Contrasts are essential because as one knows the opposite of something one can avoid the negative perception of it and find the right one for their existence. Again the example of lust, to most it is a negative contrast to love but this is not always the case. As with everything there is a positive and negative component nature.

One who achieves Zen can learn to determine what is negative, positive and what is a contrast or correspond. Life is a series of labyrinthine webs that one must navigate through one's existence. It is t the point that attainment of Zen is not only a difficult path but a narrow one.

什麼是對比？從抽象和方面來看，它們基本上是相反的反應。例如，一個人可能會體驗到抽象的慾望。它的對比可能是愛的一面，但也可能是，但它是對應。這不是唯一的反應，而只是一個例子。憤怒的動作與平靜形成對比。悲傷與快樂形成對比。對比是必不可少的，因為當一個人知道某事的反面時，一個人可以避免對它的負面看法，並找到適合他們存在的那個。另一個慾望的例子，對大多數人來說，這與愛形成了負面對比，但情況並非總是如此。與所有事物一樣，有積極和消極的成分。

達到禪的人可以學會判斷什麼是消極的，什麼是積極的，什麼是對比或對應。生活是一系列迷宮般的網絡，一個人必須在自己的存在中導航。關鍵是，冥想不僅是一條艱難的道路，而且是一條狹窄的道路。

One must keep things in perspective and by this one must be realistic. As one is in the physical plane of existence, it is only necessary that one likes and appreciates physical things. This is the natural state of things and to deprive one self of these things is this productive? In most cases it is destructive. As with any measure, extensiveness will lead to fractiousness. For example if one is attacked. Do you defend or attack yourself? The attacker is obviously influenced by one or more abstracts. It is here that your choices expand. Do you also embrace the abstracts to deal with him? Or do you embrace the aspects? Do you use the negative or the positive?? Do you elaborate on the contrasts or the corresponds? There are infinite ways with infinite results.

Keeping the aspects in perspective is called the Sanity of Values not keeping them in perspective is called the Insanity of Values

Keeping in perspective generally means keeping the abstracts and the aspects at an equal distance but not letting the abstracts overcome the aspects. An abstract kept in perspective is called a Constriction of Desires but abstracts not in perspective are called Unrestricted Constriction of Desires.

一個人必須正確看待事物，因此必須是現實的。因為人是在物質存在的層面，所以只需要喜歡和欣賞物質的東西。這是事物的自然狀態，剝奪自己這些事物是否有成效？在大多數情況下，它是破壞性的。與任何衡量標準一樣，一概而論會導致煩躁。例如，如果有人受到攻擊。你是保護自己還是攻擊自己？攻擊者顯然受到一個或多個摘要的影響。正是在這裡，您的選擇得以擴展。你也接受反對他的摘要嗎？還是你接受這些方面？你使用負數還是正數？ ?您詳細說明比較或對應關係嗎？有無限的方法，有無限的結果。

堅持觀點的觀點稱為價值理智　不堅持觀點的觀點稱為價值瘋狂

保持透視通常意味著將抽象和方面保持相等的距離，但不要讓抽象克服方面。保持透視的總結稱為慾望收縮，而非透視的總結稱為不受限制的慾望收縮。

The physical body must be strengthened as well as the mental body. The mind is the nucleus of thought and action. The body is he nucleus of reaction. To do this is called enforcement.

What is conscience? It is the spirit talking to the physical mind from the metaphysical world. How this comes about varies. It could be dreams, hallucinations or even others in tune with your person.

What is magic? Imagine the universe and all life as waves of energy and waves of possible realities. In the waves of reality are the abstracts and contrasts, both negative and positive. Magic is the interjection of another reality imposing itself between one more realities by the use various articles of speech, amulets etc.

My theories can only somewhat explain the complexities of life and hard I can be to attain true Zen. Zen waves as well as others interact and react thus producing various effects. The knowledge and observation of this is called experience.

As far as waves there are two distinct types. Aspect Wave Dominance(AWD) AND Abstract wave Dominance (ABD). Experience is a combination o always these two waves and many more but if one dominates over the other then there s a chaotic wave effect if the abstracts dominate or a Harmonic Wave

Dominance effect if the aspects dominant. It can be explained as thus,

Experience =

AWD+ABD

$$AWD^2 + ABD = HWD$$

ABD² + AWD=CWD

肉體必須加強，靈體也必須加強。頭
腦是思想和行動的核心。身體是反應
的核心。這樣做稱為強制執行。

什麼是良心？它是形而上學世界的精神和物質思
想之間的對話。這是怎麼發生的。它可能是一個
夢、幻覺，甚至是與你有關的其他東西。

什麼是魔法？將宇宙和所有生命視為能量波和可
能的現實。現實的波浪是抽象的和對比的，消極
的和積極的。魔法是對另一個現實的感嘆，它通
過使用各種語音腳本、護身符等將自己強加於另
一個現實之間。

我的理論只能在一定程度上解釋生活的複雜性，
我很難達到真正的禪宗。禪波和其他波相互作用
和反應產生各種效果。對此的認識和觀察稱為經
驗。

就波浪而言，有兩種不同的類型。縱橫波優勢
（AWD）和抽象波優勢（ABD）。經驗總是這兩種

波和更多波的組合，但如果一個波占主導地位，那麼如果抽象占主導地位，就會出現混沌波效應，如果方面占主導地位，就會出現諧波效應。可以這樣解釋，

經驗＝

四驅＋ABD

$$AWD^2 + ABD = HWD$$

$$ABD^2 + AWD = CWD$$

Outside the waves of reality exist impossibilities and improbabilities. Essentially everything and nothing in between. Between these are three phases of

EXISTENCE.

在現實的波浪之外，有不可能和不可能。基
本上一切都在兩者之間。分為三個階段
存在。

The Primary phase consists of the physical body. This
considered the part that is most understood and the most
used. This phase also the most difficult to achieve a
harmonic balance.

初級階段由身體組成。這考慮了最容
易理解和使用最多的部分。這個階段
也是最難達到諧波平衡的階段。

The Medial phase consists of the physical actions, memories
which may transcended from the primary or the final
phases As you see, each phases has it own aspects and
abstracts as well an intertwining of all three.

。中間階段包括身體運動、記憶，並且可能
超出初級或最終階段。如您所見，每個階段
都有自己的方面和抽象，以及三者的交織。

The final phase is the metaphysical phase, it is called the
final phase because as life ends this I where life goes but it
also the center of existence.

最後的階段是形而上學的階段，之所以
稱為最後階段，是因為生命結束時我生
活的地方，但它也是存在的中心。

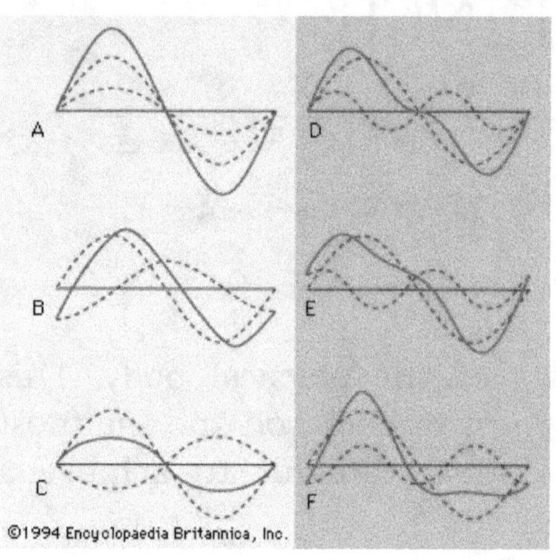

In physics there is the concept of Interference which is the net effect of the combination of two or more intersecting or coincident paths. That being said, that is always the case between levels of existence their aspects, abstracts and their perspective waves.

在物理學中有乾涉的概念，它是兩個或

多個相交或重合路徑組合的淨效應。話
雖如此，存在的層次、它們的方面、抽
象和它們的透視波之間總是如此。

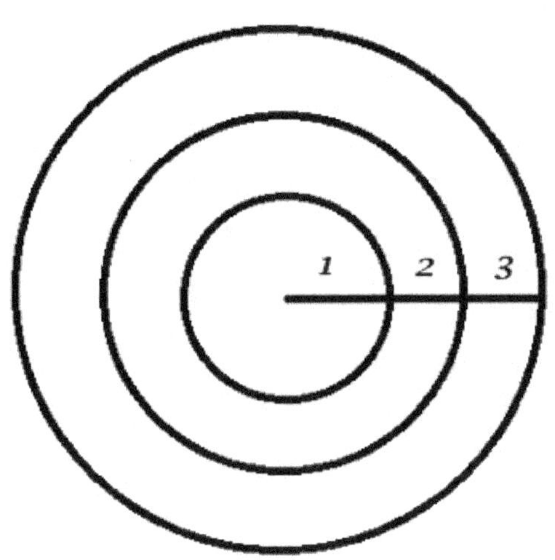

1- Final medial
2 Medial
3- Physical

-To achieve Zen one levels of existence must be concentric as shown and-in harmony.
-One must realize that all three levels have their own attributes, waves, abstracts and aspects.
-Essentially one must balance everything to achieve True Zen. The positive and the negative in all moments and points of one's life.

1- 最終內側

2 內
3-物理

- 要達到禪的層次，必須同心和諧，如圖所示。

- 必須意識到所有三個級別都有自己的屬性、波浪、摘要和方面。

- 基本上一個人必須平衡一切才能實現真正的禪宗。生活中的所有時刻和點的積極和消極

Chapter
Training

There are eight principles of training.

I- Goal Attainment- First of all you must decide what you want. If you have no destination why even start the journey?

II- Process Attainment- How will you go about succeeding in your goal. What methods or criteria will you use?

III- Reason Attainment- If you have your goal and the process, now you must have a reason for doing both.

IV- Time attainment- The fourth process is one of the most crucial. You must make the time to reach your goal and keep to this time as much as possible. Not only the when but the how long as well.

V- Refinement-. After a while you will determine and focus in other areas as you see fit. You will change days and times and even reasons, This is normal and will only help you to reach your goal.

VI- Conceptual Focus Attainment- This is just a matter of concentration fully of what your goal is while using the other steps. This process stresses equilibrium
 in the steps.

VII- Self Conversant- Who better to talk to you but yourself in matters that are important to you. You know exactly what you want and need better than anyone else.

VIII- Encirclement – Using the 7 previous steps over and over and whatever your goal is it, can be attained. How soon is up to you. How hard is up to you. YOU are the key.

章節

火車

訓練有八項原則。

I – 目標達成 – 首先你必須決定你想要什麼。如果沒有目的地，為什麼要開始旅行？

II - 過程成就 - 你將如何實現你的目標。您將使用什麼方法或標準？

III – 理性獲取 – 如果你有你的目標和你的過程，那麼現在你必須有理由同時做這兩件事。

IV - 到達時間 - 第四個過程是最關鍵的
過程之一。你必須騰出時間來實現你的
目標，並儘可能長時間地保持這個時
間。不只是什麼時候，而是多久。

V-細化-。一段時間後，您將確定並專注於您認
為合適的其他領域。你會改變日子和時間，甚至
改變原因，這很正常，只會幫助你達到目標。

VI - 達到概念焦點 - 這只是在使用其他步驟
時全神貫注的問題。這個過程強調平衡
在步驟中。

VII- 自我控制——在對你很重要的事情上，
誰比你自己更適合與你交談。你比任何人
都更清楚自己想要什麼和需要什麼。

VIII – 環繞 – 重複前面的 7 個步驟以實現您的目標。多久取決於你。這取決於你有多難。你是關鍵。

Zhāngjié

huǒchē

Chapter
Redirection

Redirection consists of two types physical and metaphysical. The ease at which one can be
 redirected depends on their willingness, sincerity, and the depth they are involving the aspects and abstracts.

Physical redirection: it consists of changing one's aspects and abstracts in the way of true positivism.
Heart: Involves controlling one's emotions and not let negativity corrupt them.
Mental: Involves not letting negative thoughts corrupt the other aspects and thus influence emotions and actions.
Spiritual: Involves essentially to not stray at allocates on the

positive which is the narrow path. In doing so the other aspects will fall into place.

章節

重定向

重定向包括物理和形而上學類型。一個人可以放心

重定向取決於他們的意願、誠意以及他們的方面和抽象的深度。

物理重定向：它涉及以真正實證主義的方式改變一個人的方面和抽象。

心：涉及控制你的情緒，而不是讓消極情緒摧毀它們。

心理：這包括不允許消極的想法擾亂其他方面，從而影響情緒和行為。

精神上的：本質上涉及不偏離正方向的分佈，即狹窄的路徑。在這樣做時，其他方面將到位。

Metaphysical redirection: Is perhaps the most important of the two. It is the hardest to maintain and to turn around from a negative path. Like the spiritual part of the physical if maintained the rest will fall into place.

What are the aspects? Three factors of both the physical and spiritual realm. Mind body and spirit. Their waves must correlate and coincide to reach a point of near contentment.

What are the abstracts? Factors that lead the aspects astray or even can strengthen them, but they must be kept in perceptive and must never overwhelm the aspects. Money; sex and power are three examples.

What are contrasts? Factors including emotions, thoughts and instincts that can be negative or positive that are simply opposites of existing factors. Anger-happy; christian-pagan; light-dark. One must be aware of the positives and negatives of everything in order to be able to understand the concept of everything.

形而上學重定向：也許是兩者中最重要的。它是最難維持的，也是最難從負面路徑中逆轉的。就像身體的精神部分一樣，如果你堅持下去，其餘的都會到位。

有哪些方面？物質和精神領域的三個因素。心靈的身體和精神。它們的波浪必須相互關聯並重合才能幾乎令人滿意。

什麼是摘要？導致相位誤入歧途的因素甚至可以加強相位，但它們必須留在感知中，永遠不能壓倒相位。錢;性和權力就是三個例子。

什麼是對比？情緒、想法和本能等因素可以是消極的或積極的，與可用的完全相反。生氣高興；基督教異教徒；弱光。為了能夠理解萬物的概念，必須了解萬物的積極和消極方面。

When on reaches the point of equilibrium(POE), where everything is totally balanced or nearly. Then one must maintain this balance which will not be easy. The task to reach to reach is not easy and the task to maintain will not be easy either.

What is the shock-wave or the Titanic wave? This is a position or situation in ones life where they realize that they must do or die. It is a point where the aspects or in the background and the abstracts dominate. I is a point where there is no equilibrium of the positive but only the negative. Eventually this wave will cripple a person and break them down until they are sinking into the abyss of what hey were. At this point, redirection is the key.

What are vestiges? These are remnants of ancestors or generations or even past happenings that can influence the aspects. Again they can be positive or negative. They can exist in memory or reality. Vestiges are a different waves all together by themselves.

當達到平衡點 （POE） 時，一切都完美平衡或接近平衡點。然後必須保持這種平衡，這並不容易。到達的任務不容易，維護的任務也不容易。

什麼是衝擊波或泰坦尼克波？這是一個人生活中的一個位置或情況，他們意識到他們必須做或死。這是方面或背景和抽象占主導地位的一點。I 是一個沒有正平衡而只有負平衡的點。最終，這波浪潮會削弱一個人並壓垮他們，直到他們沉入曾經的深淵。此時，重定向是關鍵。

什麼是遺跡？這些是祖先或世代的殘餘，可以影響方面甚至過去發生的事情。同樣，它們可以是積極的或消極的。它們可以存在於記憶或現實中。廢墟本身就是不同的波浪。

The All-knowing Ghost

There once was a wife who became ill and on her last moments made her husband promise not see or love any other woman but her. If he did do such a thing, she would come back as a specter and haunt him the rest of his life.

For several years he did as he promised until one day he found someone that he could not keep from loving and seeing. After he proposed to her, that very night the image of his deceased wife appeared in front his bed. She yelled at him for not keeping the promise he made. Thereafter, every night she haunted him about the promise. The specter reminded him of the life he had with his wife and everything that he done so far with the woman that was soon to be his wife. Verbatim,per every action the specter, knew in detail. It was too much for the man and so he sought out the help of the Guru.

"This ghost of yours is very cleaver and knowledgeable." the guru said after listening to his tale of woe. Getting up from his mediating position he goes over to whisper in the man's ear as to what to the next time the specter arrives.

That evening as usual the specter appeared and started her usual tirade but this time the man listened and waited until the specter was finished.
"Wise ghost of my wife. You are right about everything you say and you know everything it seems. Answer me one question and will continue to keep the promise I made to you."
"Ask your question husband." the specter replied.
Grabbing a handful grain of rice that were in a bag next to his bed he asked.

"How many grains of rice do I have in my hand?' Upon hearing the question. The specter dissipated before the man's eyes to be gone forever. Why couldn't the ghost tell him the answer to his question?

Like a Bell

A young lad went up to the guru and asked. How should prepare himself for whatever question he asks and what ever answer he may receive.
"I am a bell to you, the guru replied. "If you just tap me you will only get a ping but if you strike with all you have thing the nose will deafen your ears.

像鐘聲

一個年輕的小伙子走到大師面前問道。如何準備他提出的任何問題以及他可能收到的任何答案。"我是你的鈴鐺，"大師回答。"如果你只是輕敲我，你只會得到一個 ping，但如果你用你所有的東西輕敲，鼻子會聾你的耳朵。"

Hunting Two Deer

A student of the martial way comes up to the guru with a question.
"I wish to learn from you guru but also from another teacher. What do you think of this?
If you hunt two deer at once, the guru replied, you will either chase one, catch one or starve."

狩獵兩隻鹿

一個武林弟子向師父提問。

"我想向你師父學習，又想向別的老師學習，你怎麼看？

師父回答說，如果你同時殺死兩隻鹿，你要么追一隻，要么抓一隻，要么餓死。"

Strength and Power
Concentration and focus

After winning several feats of strength, a young man challenged the guru. He was indeed strong by pulling up trees with is bare hands and bending steel.
"Okay, now is your turn guru let's see how strong you are." The guru bowed and simply walked over to the tree the young man pulled and grabbed and put it back into the ground where it came from. The steel bar that was bent, he bent back into its original shape and then wrapped it around the very tree he just replanted.
"You are very strong but you lack power. You are very skilled but you lack focus. You are very young but you lack concentration.

力量和力量

專注和專注

在贏得了幾次力量壯舉之後，一個年輕人挑戰了上師。徒手拔樹，彎鋼，他確實很強壯。

"好了，現在輪到你的上師了，看看你有多強。"古魯鞠了一躬，然後簡單地走到樹前，年輕人拉起一隻手，抓住它，把它放回原處。彎曲的鋼筋，他將鋼筋彎曲回原來的形狀，並纏繞在他剛剛重新種植的樹上。

"你很強大，但你缺乏力量。你很熟練，但你缺乏專注。你年輕，但你缺乏專注。

Tale of the Coin

There was a great battle, a general wanted to attack the enemy even though their numbers were twice his. He was adamant but his men wanted him to see the guru first. He complied and the guru bowed and pulled out a coin.

"Great general we shall see if your confidence is enough to conquer the tides of face. You will flip this coin and if it lands on the dragon side you will you will win and if lands on the sword side you will lose.

The general threw the coin in the air and watched as it landed on the ground. It was the dragon side and everyone cheered for themselves and their upcoming victory because of the confidence. After the battle the general returned to the guru and bowed.

"It was destiny that I won! "

"Quite right you are general," the guru remarked showing him the coin he threw which had both sides as dragons....

硬幣故事

在一場大戰中，一個將軍想要攻擊敵人，即使他們的數量是他的兩倍。他很固執，但他的手下想讓他先見上師。他照辦了，上師一鞠躬，取出一枚硬幣。

"將軍，看你的信心是否足夠強大，能戰勝面子的潮水。你擲硬幣，如果落在龍的一邊，你就贏了，如果落在劍的一邊，你就贏了。會輸。

將軍把硬幣扔到空中，看著它掉到地上。這是龍的一面，每個人都為自己和即將到來的勝利歡呼，因為有信心。

戰鬥結束後，將軍回到大師面前行禮。

"我命中註定要贏！"

"是的，你是將軍，"上師說，把他扔的硬幣給他看，硬幣的兩面都有龍……

The Ant and the Horse

There were a group of students who wished to converse with guru.
The guru was meditating in an open field. One of the students sat
down in front of him and simply asked
"What is Zen?
The guru opened one eye.
"Is that all?" the student asked.
The guru opened his other eye.
The student stood up and bowed and walked away.
Another student walked forward in front his peers.
"Did any of you understand that?"
They all shook their heads confused.
The second student then turned to the guru.
"Great guru you must TELL us what Zen is."
"If you wish words," the guru replied, then Zen is simply an ant
riding a horse."

螞蟻和馬

有一群學生希望與大師交談。古魯在開闊的田野
中冥想。一個學生在他面前坐下，簡短地問道

"什麼是禪？

古魯睜開了一隻眼睛。

"就這樣？"學生問。

古魯睜開了另一隻眼睛。

學生站起身來，鞠躬離開。

另一個學生走在他的同齡人面前。

"你們有誰明白嗎？"

他們都疑惑的搖搖頭。

第二個學生然後轉向上師。

"大師，您一定要告訴我們什麼是禪。"

"如果你想說話，"大師答道，那麼禪就是馬背上的螻蟻。

Enlightenment

One morning it was heard that a young man had achieved enlightenment. This was caused for excitement. Other villagers went to the young man to see for themselves." Is it true have you achieved enlightenment?"
"Yes it is true."
"Well how do you feel?"
"The same as I always do just more alive."

啟示

一天早上，我聽說一個年輕人開悟了。這是出於興奮。其他村民親自去見年輕人。 "你真的開悟了嗎？"

"是的，這是真的。"

"那你感覺如何？"

"就像我一直做的那樣，只是有更多的能量。"

Total Knowing

After a decade of training and meditation, a young monk became a master in his own right. One rainy day he decided to visit the guru. As soon as he walked in the guru had 3 questions:
How many steps did he take to get here? 123
How many breaths did to take to get here? 16 breaths
How many raindrops fell between when started and when you got here? The new master did not know the answer. So he bowed and only returned when he did now the answer.

全知

經過十年的修行和禪修，一位年輕的僧人憑藉自己的能力成為了大師。一個下雨天，他決定去拜訪師父。一走進上師，他就有3個問題：

他走了多少步才到這裡？123

需要多少呼吸才能到達這裡？16次呼吸

從一開始直到你到達這裡，有多少雨滴落下？新主人不知道答案。所以他鞠了一躬，現在才回答。

Old vs. Young

There was an old warrior. Even though he was up in his years he was still very good at the martial arts. His reputation grew and many came to learn from him.

One day another warrior came to the village, but this warrior was very young and strong. He reason was visiting was to beat the old master. Not only was the young warrior strong and fast but he had an unnatural ability to see the weakness in any opponent and so when they made the first move he always won

The old warrior gladly accepted the challenge and two met in the center of the village for their fight. The young warrior shouted insults of all degrees at the old warrior and even spit and threw dirt at him, but the old warrior did and said nothing and just waited. Finally the young warrior could not wait any longer and attacked the old warrior, but he had exhausted him himself with is insults and bantering so he was not as fast as he usually was. The young was simply defeated by a mere dodge and push to the ground. The young warrior said nothing and left ashamed.

The old warriors students were dispirited that their master did not strike him into the ground and asked.
"Why did you take the insults and then finally just move and push him down?"
"Why waste energy on the wasteful? Why taste dirt if you do not like sand?
Why draw blood when blood already flows?:"

老人與年輕人

有退伍軍人。雖然年紀大了，但武術還是很厲害的。他的名氣越來越大，很多人都來向他學習。有一天，村里又來了一位武士，但這位武士年輕而強壯。他此行的目的，就是要打敗老者。這位年輕的鬥士不僅強壯敏捷，而且他有一種不自然的能力，可以看到任何對手的弱點，所以當他們邁出第一步時，他總是能贏。

老武士欣然接受了挑戰，兩人在村子中央相遇，展開廝殺。年輕武者對著老武者大吼大叫，甚至吐口水、扔泥土，但老武者沒有說話，只是等著。終於，年輕武者迫不及待，向老武者發起了攻擊，但老武者被他的謾罵和戲弄已經筋疲力盡，速度也沒有平時那麼快。青年身形一閃，直接被推倒在地。年輕的武士一言不發地離開了。那些老武者學員因為師父沒有將他打倒在地而惱火，紛紛問道。

"你為什麼接受了侮辱，然後只是移動並將他推倒？"

"為什麼要把你的精力浪費在浪費上？如果你不喜歡沙子，為什麼要試試泥土？

血已經在流了，為什麼還要抽血？:"

The Flow

There was a story of how the guru watched another monk fall into a river which lead to a waterfall. Everyone looking thought that he would drown but somehow he survived the waterfall and was found downstream. People asked him how did he survive and he didn't know but the guru walked up to him with a blanket and relied," He did not drown in the water because he became the water and flowed as water does. Water does not harm itself.

流動

有一個故事，上師如何看到另一個僧侶掉進通往瀑布的河流中。每個人都認為他會淹死，但不知何故，他從瀑布中倖存下來，並在下游被發現。人們問他是怎麼活下來的，他不知道，但師父拿著毯子走到他身邊，靠在他身上說：“他沒有淹死在水里，因為他變成了水，像水一樣流動。不要傷害自己。

A Copycat

When he asked about Zen, the guru one day replied simply," yes". A young boy watching

 decided to copy the actions of the guru, so that when around asked about Zen he would go," Yes"

The guru heard abut his little copycat and caught him one day in the act. The boy was scared at the what might happen to him. The guru with a blank expression on his face simply said,"No"

The boy out of habit simply said, "Yes," The guru then bowed and walked away from the boy who was now smiling.

模仿者

當他問起禪時，有一天，上人簡單地回答
說：「是的。」一個小男孩在看
　決定複製上師的行為，這樣當有人問禪時，他
會說，「是的」
大師聽到了他的小模仿者的聲音，有一天抓住了
他的動作。男孩被可能發生在他身上的事情嚇壞
了。師父面無表情地說：「沒有。」
男孩習慣性地說：「是的。」古魯鞠了一躬，從微
笑的男孩身邊走開。

A Visit

Word of the guru had spread and a man from a village far away wanted to see this wise man. Upon reaching the place where the guru was there was an older man who met him at the door.
"I am here to see the wise man guru." He said to the older man.

The older smiled and brought him inside, as they walked through he saw many things but not the guru. Before he realized it he was walking out the door and outside again.

"Where is the guru? I wish to learn from him!"

"You have already met him as you walked through the house and you have met e. Any one you meet in life however insignificant or boring or mundane.. see them as a guru. If you can do this then you will learn more than you ever realize."

Royalty

A member of the royal court was visiting the people and saw the guru. She bowed and he bowed in return.

"Great guru," she asked. "What is the most profound statement you can tell me?"

"Nothing is everything; Everything is something, something is nothing."

"But if this is true, then something is everything"

"If you know that and this then I can teach you nothing. That is the profoundness you are looking for." and the guru bowed.

版税

一位皇室成員正在拜訪人們，並看到了大師。她鞠躬，他也鞠躬回報。

"偉大的主人，"她問道。 "你能告訴我的最深刻的陳述是什麼？"

"沒有就是一切；一切都是，也沒有什麼。"

"但如果這是真的，那一切都是什麼"

"如果你知道這個和這個，那我什麼都教不了。這就是你要找的深度。"大師鞠躬。

Words

There was a monastery that had a vow silence, but once year they could speak three words. The guru visited one day this year and ask a monk what he would like to say.

"Bed...not...soft.." said one monk

"M mm.." said the guru. And the guru left the monastery and return eight years later to asked the same monk again.

"Food...tastes..terrible...."

"I see," said the guru. And again he left to come back a third year to the same monk.

"I will quit.." the monk answered when asked.

"No wonder," the guru replied. "all you do is waste words.."

Knowing

One day the guru and a fellow monk were walking the river.
"Look at the fish jumping and swimming have so much fun with themselves." the guru said.
"You are not a fish, so how can you know that they are enjoying themselves?" the fellow monk asked.
"You are not me, so how do you know that I do not know that the fish are enjoying themselves?"the guru asked backed.
The fellow monk was caught off by the question and had no response...

會心
有一天，上師和一個僧人在河邊散步。
"你看魚在潛水和游泳時玩得很開心，"主人說。
"你不是魚，你怎麼知道他們玩得很開心？"發起人問道。
"你不是我，你怎麼知道我不知道魚兒玩的開心？"師父反問。

和尚一頭霧水，沒有回答……

Learning the Art

The son of a great warrior went to his father and ask the learn the art of bravery. The father agreed and that night he took him to a local tavern to eat and drink. While they were drinking, the father three a cup of rice wine at a nearby patron and pointed at his son. Saying good luck he went outside the tavern and went home. Hours later, his son returned home bloodied and exhausted.

"Father," he yelled angrily." Why did you throw the wine, blame and then leave me? If it was for fear of getting beaten up I wouldn't have made it out alive. It everything I had to get back home!"

The father smiled.

"Son, you could have left with me but that would been safer, instead you stayed and fought outnumbered out of fear and desperation. That was your first lesson in the art of bravery.

Masterpiece

The was a skilled artist in a village where everyone gathered around to watch him paint. One day the guru walked by and the artist showed his newest painting.

"It's okay." was all the guru said and kept walking.

The next day the artist had another painting ready for when the guru walked by.

"Not bad." was all the guru said and kept walking again.

Infuriated, the artist tried to think of something that would catch the guru's attention.

On the third day, the artist still had nothing drawn and the guru walked by and stopped.

"Now that is a masterpiece." he said and bowed and walked off yet again.

傑作

他是一個村子裡的熟練藝術家，每個人都聚在一起看他畫畫。有一天，大師路過，畫家展示了他的最新畫作。

"沒關係。"師父說了這麼多，繼續說下去。

第二天，師父經過時，畫家又準備了一幅畫。

"不錯。"師父就這麼說了，接著說。

憤怒的藝術家試圖想出一些能引起大師注意的東西。

第三天，畫家還沒畫完，師父就走過去停了下來。

"它現在是一件傑作，"他說，鞠了一躬，然後離開了。

Perhaps

There was a skilled farmer who had worked many years and one day his best horse ran away. His neighbors came by to give their regrets for what happened.

"Such terrible fortune" they said.

"Perhaps." the farmer replied.

A few days later the same horse returned with several other wild horses.

"What great fortune!" the neighbors replied.

"Perhaps." the farmer replied.

The next day his son tried to ride one the wild horses and broke his arm.

"Such bad fortune" they said.

"Perhaps." was all the farmer said.

The next day the military men came to draft young men but upon seeing his son injured they did not draft him.

"Indeed such how great things turned out for you!" they said.

"PERHAPS." was all the farmer said.

<u>When More is not Enough</u>

Once there was a stonemason who was dissatisfied with his lot in life. He walked past the home of a wealthy trader one day. People were coming to him and he had lavish things.
" How powerful this trader is, I wish I was like him. One moment later, he was a trader enjoying the same things he had just seen and detested by those lesser than him.

當更多還不夠時

從前，有一個石匠對自己的命運不滿意。一天，他路過一位富商的家。人們來找他，他有奢侈品。

"這個交易員有多強，我希望我能像他一樣。片刻之後，他是一個交易員，享受他剛剛看到的東西，以及比他小的人討厭的東西。

A government official came by after a while, carried in a chair by several men in the air. Behind him were men beating on bells and gongs and singing his praises. No matter how well off they were, all had to bow to him when he came by.

I wish I were like him." Again he was given his way and was carried around like a slave, and people hated his status more than when he was a trader, but this was a hot summer day and he looked up at the sun.

I'd love to be the sun, how powerful it is as it shines over us!

He became the very sun, shining light and heat upon everyone, and even burning the forests and crops. He was hated more than he ever disliked the things he wishes to become; but as he lavished in his power, a pitch-black gloom of a cloud came over him.

"How almighty this darkness is to block out the very sun! I wish I was this cloud."

Then he became the very cloud and rain upon the ground, flooding everything from crops to villages and making everyone, even more, hate him.

But then he was suddenly being pushed away by some invisible force, and he saw that it was the

不一會兒，一個政府官員走了過來，被

幾個人抬到椅子上，懸在半空。他身後

是敲鐘鑼鼓歌頌他的人。再好，他來

的時候，每個人都要向他鞠躬。

我希望我能像他一樣。　　"他又被給了他的路，

像奴隸一樣被帶走，人們比他做生意時更討厭他

的身份，但那是一個炎熱的夏天，他抬頭看著太

陽。

我很想成為太陽，它照耀著我們多麼強大！

他變成了太陽，將光和熱照耀在每個人身上，甚至燒毀了森林和莊稼。他比以往任何時候都更討厭自己想要成為的樣子。可就在他舒展筋骨的時候，一團烏雲籠罩了他。

"這黑暗阻擋太陽的力量是多麼強大！我希望我是這片雲。"

然後他變成了地上的雲雨，淹沒了從莊稼到村莊的一切，讓所有人，更加恨他。

可就在這時，他突然被一股無形的力量推開，他看到那是

wind.

"How almighty is the wind that it van push the rain cloud away. I want to be the wind! "

And so he became the very wind, blowing the hats off heads and the tiles and bricks from homes. Blowing the sails of ships and hated even more so still than before but, after a while, he ran into something that he could not push, no matter how hard he blew upon it. He saw that it was a huge rock.

"How might this huge rock is to handle the breath of the very wind. I want to become this rock! "

When he was a rock, he saw the sound of something breaking him down, and he felt himself changing. Who could have done this to him, the almighty rock? What could have been more powerful than I?

He glanced down to see a stonemason standing below him...

風。

"風好大，把雨雲都吹走了。我要成為風！"

於是他變成了風，吹掉了他頭上的帽子，吹走了房子的瓷磚和磚塊。吹著風帆，他比以前更討厭了，可是過了一會兒，他遇到了一個吹多少也推不開的東西。他看到那是一塊巨大的石頭。

"這塊巨石怎麼能承受風的氣息，我要變成這塊石頭！"

當他還是一塊石頭的時候，他看到有什麼東西壓在他身上的聲音，他感覺自己在變。誰能對他，萬能的磐石做出這樣的事？還有什麼能比我強？他低頭一看，下面站著一個石匠……

The Greatest Lesson

A famous monk had learned his greatest lesson one day by

spending 30 years in the forest. When he walked out, he had learned from himself that Zen was NOT his own mind and walked the land telling everyone what he had learned.

One day he met the guru who has retreated to learn the secret of Zen.

The guru asked, "Fellow monk, what did you learn while you were in the forest?"

"Ah!,great guru I have learned the Zen is NOT your mind. Now what did you learn?"

"Fellow monk, but I learned that Zen WAS my mind..."

最大的教訓

一位著名的僧侶在森林裡度過了 30 年的一天，他學到了他最大的教訓。出門後，他自知禪非自心，走遍天下，將所學之事告訴大家。

有一天，他遇到了一位上師，他已經閉關學習禪宗的秘密。

師問："和尚，你在森林裡學到了什麼？"

"啊！大師，我知道禪不是你的心，現在你學到了什麼？"

"和尚，但我知道禪是我的心……"

<u>What is Moving?</u>

Two men having a philosophical discussion about clothing on a line as they drank.
"It's the clothing that's moving." one man said.
"No, it is the wind that is moving." the other man said.
The guru walks by and the two men called to him and asked him what he thought.
"It is simple... it is your mind that is moving.." he bowed and continued on his journey.

什麼是手機？
兩個男人一邊喝酒一邊對著裝進行哲學討論。
"是衣服在動，"一個男人說。
"不，風在移動，"另一個人說。
古魯走過來，兩個人攔住了他，問他怎麼想。
"很簡單……是你的心在動……" 他躬身繼續前行。

<u>Nature</u>

Two monks were walking and saw a wounded mam. One them helped and the man was a thief and robbed him and ran away. They continued on and saw another wounded man and the same monk helped and was robbed again. This happen three times and his fellow asked him.
"Why do you continue to help this men when you know they will rob you/"
"Because," the monk replied," to help is my nature."

自然

兩個和尚走著，看見了一個受傷的母親。他們幫助了一個小偷，搶劫了他並逃跑了。他們繼續前行，看到另一個受傷的人，在同一個僧人的幫助下，再次搶劫。這種情況發生了三遍，他的同伴問他。

"你知道這些人會搶劫你，為什麼還要繼續幫助他們/"
"因為，"僧人回答，"我的天性就是幫助。"

Questions

A famous thinker once asked the guru how did help people.
"I help them by having them not able to ask me any more questions…" Then he bowed.

一位著名的思想家曾問師父如何幫助人。
"我幫助他們，這樣他們就不能再問我任何問題了……" 然後他鞠了一躬。

Not Yet

The guru was summoned by a king and asked.
"What happens to you guru and enlightened man after death?"
"How would I know the answer to that king? The guru replied.
"Because you are the guru that's why." answered the king.
"Yes, but I am not yet a dead guru and so the questioned cannot be answered."

還沒有

上師被國王召見並詢問。

"你的上師和成道者死後會怎樣？"

"我怎麼會知道那個國王的答案？大師答道。

"因為你是大師，這就是為什麼。"國王回答。

"是的，但我還不是死去的上師，所以無法回答問題。"

The Present

A warrior was captured by his enemy and thrown into prison. Night came but he could not sleep for fear of what would happen

to him. But then he had remembered the words of the guru one day as he was riding by a village.
"Tomorrow does not exist yet and so it is an illusion of time. Whereas the present is now and a reality." Remembering those words he bowed to where though the guru would be and fell into a peaceful sleep.

現在

一個戰士被他的敵人俘虜並投入監獄。夜幕降臨，他卻因害怕會發生什麼事而無法入睡。但是有一天，當他騎馬穿過一個村莊時，他想起了他主人的話。

"明天還不存在，所以這是時間的幻覺。現在它已成為現實。"想起那些話，他向上師所在的地方鞠躬，然後睡著了。

Cherish

A wealthy man once asked the guru to write something down that his fail would cherish after he was gone.. n a large scroll the guru simply wrote.
"Back and Forth."

When the wealthy man so it, he was quite angry.
"Guru I asked you to write something my family would cherish after I'm gone. Why did you write something so simple as this? And how would they cherish this?
"Back and forth, To go forward one must think back. If they saw how good you were to them and to others that alone will propel them forward at your pace or even better. I have given you what you asked for and he bowed and walked away leaving the merchant ashamed.

珍惜

有位富人曾經請他的上師寫下一些他在失敗後會珍惜的東西。在一個大捲軸上，上師簡單地寫著。

"來回。"

財主這麼一說，就生氣了。

"師父，我讓你寫一些我走了以後家人會珍惜的東西，你怎麼寫的這麼簡單？他們怎麼會珍惜？

"要來回走，要往前走，你必須反省。如果他們看到你對他們和其他人有多好，那將推動他們以你的速度前進，甚至更好。我給了你你的東西要求，他鞠躬走開，對商人感到羞恥。

<u>Calmness</u>

There once was a huge storm of rain and thunder and lightning. The people were terrified but the guru was there and led them to a safe place. After the storm had passed the guru finally spoke.
"Now you have seen calmness in the face of adversity, I did not panic as you did, my calmness calmed you. I led you to safety and all will be well. Despite what you saw I was somewhat tense which you might have seen as drank a big glass of lemon juice which you saw me clearly drink..
A small child in the group started giggling while the guru spoke.
"Why do you laugh little one? The guru asked.
"Because silly that wasn't lemon juice that was just plain water!"
The guru bowed to the child and smiled.
"It seems I wasn't the only in a state of composure."

冷靜的

曾經有一場巨大的暴雨和閃電。人們嚇壞了，但古魯在那裡，把他們帶到了一個安全的地方。風雨過後，師父終於開口了。

"現在你在逆境中看到了平靜，我沒有像你那樣恐慌，我的平靜讓你平靜下來。我把你帶到了安全的地方，一切都會好起來的。雖然你看到我有點緊張，但你可能已經看到了一個大玻璃檸檬汁，你看到我明顯喝了..

當主人說話時，小組中的一個孩子開始咯咯地笑。

"小傢伙怎麼笑了？師父問道。

"因為愚蠢的不是檸檬汁而是白開水！"

大師向孩子鞠躬微笑。

"看來我不是唯一一個處於沉著狀態的人。"

Code of Silence

There were four monks who decided silent mediation for three weeks. One night while meditating the candles went out and the

1st monk said,
"My goodness! The candles just all went our!"
The 2nd monk said:
"Ssh.. we aren't supposed to be talking!."
The 3rd monk said:
"Hey! remember the code of silence! "
The 4th monk said:
"It's the a good thing I'm the only that didn't say a word..."

沉默守則

四位和尚決定打坐三個星期。一天晚上，在打坐時，蠟燭熄滅了，第一個和尚說：

"我的天哪！蠟燭已經飛到我們這裡了！"

第二個和尚說：

"噓……我們不該說話！"

第三個和尚說：

"嘿！記住無聲密碼！"

四和尚說：

"幸好我是唯一一個不說話的人……"

Demon

Once there was a monk that while he was meditation saw a four legged dark beast breathing fire in front of him. Each day as he meditated it would closer and bigger. He became frighted and went to the guru. He was ready to kill it it was necessary but the guru shook his head as in a no. Instead he told the monk to tell the demon to breathe its fire on him. The monk was wary but trusted the guru, again the demon and appeared and the monk told him to breath its fire. The demon did and then disappeared.

The next day the monk returned to guru to tell him what happened and the guru said OK now lift up your shirt. The monk did as he was told ans aw that he had burn marks from a fire. The guru bowed to the monk and walked away.

惡魔

從前有一個僧人正在打坐，突然看到一隻四足的黑色野獸在他面前噴火。隨著他每天冥想，它會越來越近。他嚇壞了，去找大師。他正要殺了它，這是必要的，但大師不贊成地搖了搖頭。相反，他告訴和尚告訴惡魔向他噴火。和尚小心翼翼，但相信上師，惡魔又出現了，和尚叫他噴火。惡魔做到了，然後消失了。

第二天，比丘回到上師那裡，告訴他發生了什麼事，上師說是的，現在掀起你的襯衫。和尚照他說的做了，結果身上有燒傷的痕跡。師父向僧人鞠躬，轉身離去。

<u>Prose</u>

Words like fire
Burning on a pyre
puts the world ablaze
Setting the eyes upon a bowlful gaze
The yin and the yang
A thousand lifetimes
Aging like wine
Baked like swine
A thousand rhymes
Hymns for the choir
Words like fire

To pace

for a race
do you walk
or do you run
Are you serious
Are do you make fun
Always a fire
How it burns potent
Always your desire

A Place

There is within a place
That is full of peace
and no pain
but lots of rain
A place where any touch
is always good and never it seems too much
Beyond horrors
Not beyond hopes
This is place is yours
and you have the keys
No need to ask
No need for pleas
One moment that is right

Be it day or be it night
This place is yours if you can stand its light...

Bloom into your color
Be a flower
Grow
Do not stop
Do not rot
A flower
A weed
Both come from a motherly seed

A poet of lemon and wine
tis not of ease

nor too hard
But a poet is poet
And a bard is a bard
To tease and to urge
To release and to purge
With word and pen
Like an egg to a hen
To share poetic thoughts
To open the songbook of life
So you can sing your song
The purpose of poet is a long list indeed
A poet of rice and wine
Tis not of cheese
But of rice
The taste so nice
Such purpose...to breed

For passion
A search
On the highest mountains perch
To the bed of the sea
A net is out what will you catch
Enough to fill or enough to thrill?
Are you a climber or a fisherman?
The nature of both is to achieve

One is a job and the other is just to believe…

To awaken
Look and the stars and the sun
To awaken
Then your journey has just begun
Remember where you started
Remember where you are
Remember the distance between the two
Is closer than you think
No matter how far along you are…

A deafening world
Where peace is hated

but yet created
Without it there would be no war
The yin and the yang
The hope and the fear
Such a loud world
Hearing peace through it all
quite clear/....

<u>Ponderings</u>

There was a notorious thief that was brought in front of a clever judge.
' I will teach you something, you thief that you do not know the concept of. I hear you always manage to get yourself out of jail on some technicality. You are sentenced to death of course but I will give you one chance to stay your execution. Simply state in front of me one true testimony and you will not be hanged but instead, serve jail time, but if your statement is deemed false you will be hanged until dead. No sentences of metaphysics or abstracts will get you out of this predicament. Now return to your cell and when you are ready, the court will be waiting.
What did the thief say to the judge?

有一個臭名昭著的小偷被帶到一位聰明的法官面前。
"我會教你一些東西，你這個不懂這個概念的小偷。我聽說你總是設法在一些技術問題上讓自己出獄。你當然被判處死刑，但我會給你機會繼續執行。你不會被絞死，而是服刑，但如果你的陳述被發現是虛假的，你就會被絞死。沒有任何形而上學或抽象的句子能讓你擺脫這種困境。現在回到你的牢房，當你準備好時，法庭會等待。

小偷對法官說了什麼？

Tony learned from Jack on how to be a lawyer for free until get gets his first case and succeeds in winning the case. But he decides he doesn't want to be a lawyer but a trainer and never pays Tony back. Tony then decides to ask for his the money instead, but Jack refuses and so Tony sues him.

Tony thinks that if Jack loses, then he wins and he gets his money and if jack wins then Tony still wins because he wins his first case.

But Jack thinks that if he loses then he doesn't have pay since he didn't fulfill the original agreement and even if he wins the original contract is void since he won and doesn't have to pay anyway.

Whose is righter than right?

托尼向杰克學習如何免費成為一名律師，直到他拿到第一個案子並贏得了官司。但他決定他不想成為一名律師而是一名培訓師，並且永遠不會回報托尼。然後托尼決定向他要錢，但傑克拒絕了，所以托尼起訴了他。

托尼認為，如果傑克輸了，他就贏了，他得到了他的錢，如果傑克贏了，那麼托尼仍然贏了，因為他贏了他的第一個案子。

但傑克認為，如果他輸了，那麼他是沒有報酬的，因為他沒有履行原來的協議，即使他贏了，原來的合同也是無效的，因為他贏了，無論如何也不必支付。

Two boys were caught climbing out of the school's bathroom window. The principal tells them to confess to smoking in the boy's room but they will not. The principal sends one boy and tells the other to sit down

"John, he says, "it will be better for you if just admit to everything, then if you do you will not get suspended but instead a much lighter punishment"

"But I didn't do it," says John.

"Well, if you didn't do anything, you have nothing to fear, but if Joe tells me that the both of you were smoking then you will be kicked out of school! Now leave and tell Joe to come in and that will give you time to think about what I've said.

Joe comes in and the principal says the same thing verbatim to

him. He leaves to think in different rooms for a time.
What can John say to help himself out whether or not he did anything or not?

兩名男孩被抓獲從學校浴室的窗戶爬出。校長讓他們承認在男孩的房間裡吸煙，但他們不肯。
校長派了一個男孩，讓另一個坐下
"約翰，他說，'你最好承認一切都會對你更好，如果你承認了，你就不會被停職，你會受到較輕的懲罰
"但我沒有那樣做，"約翰說。
"好吧，如果你什麼都不做，你也沒什麼好怕的，但如果喬告訴我你們都在抽煙，你會被學校開除的！現在走，告訴喬進來，它會讓你有時間思考我說的話。
喬進來了，校長一字不差地對他說了同樣的話。
他離開在另一個房間裡想了一會兒。
不管他有沒有做過什麼，約翰能說些什麼來幫助自己擺脫困境？

<u>Pop Quiz</u>

One spring's day a professor told his class there would be a pop quiz on everything they had learned the entire year and if they passed it they would pass for the year regardless of their current grade. He was then asked when the pop quiz and he answered. "That's why it's a pop quiz, you won't know when it will pop up but I'll give you a clue. I will give it to you between now and the end of the semester," That's no answer!!" they exclaimed. "Is it really?", the professor pondered.

After the class, Susie and Sam are talking about the quiz. "If I knew what day it was on then I know when to study harder to memorize everything right before the quiz. Susie said. "Aha!,. Don't freak out I don't think there will be a pop quiz because it's not logical if you think about it. Sam replied. "Are you nuts why would say that. He just told us to expect the unexpected!" Susie exclaimed. Sam started to explain his theory: "That the test couldn't be tomorrow or the last day of class since sine those were days we would expect. "So, tomorrow and the last day are out but still leaves a few in between." "Yeah so if we rule out the days close to today and the days close to the last day that's two weeks that we know can have a pop quiz." "So if we know it can this week or the last week then we will know it's the middle week and not a surprise so there cant be a pop quiz! I see your logic. We are good to go! "

The two students don't tell anyone else what they figured out and smiled as everyone else studied and crammed like crazy. Then one day about a week afterward the original declaration the professor starts handing out papers for the quiz.
"Wait! You cant do this professor!" shouted Susie.
"Why not?" says the professor.
"Because you said a pop quiz that we wouldn't expect and so you cant give us that we do expect. Wait you cant give us a surprise quiz when we expect a surprise quiz.
"But you are not expecting the quiz today and so it is as I said." stated the professor smiling.

Who was right?

突擊測驗

一個春天的一天，一位教授告訴他的班級會有一個關於他們一整年學到的所有知識的小測驗，如果他們通過了，無論他們目前的成績如何，他們都會通過這一年。然後他被問到什麼時候彈出測驗，他回答了。

"這就是為什麼它是一個流行測驗，你不知道它什麼時候會彈出，但我會給你一個線索。從現在到學期結束，我會給你，"那是沒有答案的！！"他們驚嘆道。

"真的嗎？"教授沉思著。

下課後，蘇西和山姆正在討論測驗。

"如果我知道今天是哪一天，那麼我就知道什麼時候該更努力地學習，以便在測驗前記住所有內容。蘇茜說。

"啊哈！，。不要驚慌我不認為會有一個流行測驗，因為如果你考慮一下它是不合邏輯的。山姆回答。

"你瘋了為什麼會這麼說。他只是告訴我們要預料到意想不到的事情！"蘇茜驚呼道。

山姆開始解釋他的理論：

"考試不可能是明天或上課的最後一天，因為那是我們所期望的日子。

"所以，明天和最後一天已經結束了，但中間還有一些。"

"是的，所以如果我們排除接近今天的日子和接近結束的日子，也就是兩週，我們知道可能會有一個小測驗。"

"所以如果我們知道這週或上週沒問題，那麼我們就會知道這是周中而不是驚喜，所以不會有測驗！我明白你的邏輯。我們可以走了！"

兩個學生沒有告訴任何人他們的想法，笑著看著其他人瘋狂地學習和收拾東西。大約一周後的一天，教授開始分發測驗試卷。

"等等！你不可能是這個教授！"蘇茜喊道。

"為什麼不？"教授說。

"因為你說了一個我們沒想到的測驗，所以你不能給我們我們期望的東西。等等，當我們期待一個驚喜測驗時，你不能給我們一個驚喜測驗。

"不過你沒想到今天會有小測驗，所以就像我說的那樣，"教授笑著說。

The mind's eye
Living in the past
Such sight for future will carry and like rice last
Suffering of time
Sands of time
Scars of time
Joy in the heart
Never leaves just covered
Looking back at the dark
And you will see only darkness
Looking back at the light
Joy in heart

Always there
Even when smothered

Pen and paper
Keyboard and screen
Best friends I have
Even if no else has seen
Exploding words
Volcanic coals
Erupting goals
A sigh of relief
The release of stress
Pen and paper
Keyboard and screen
Showing the fear and grief
Making it less

Which Toy?

There was a great toy maker and he built a special toy ship for a little boy at the request of his father. The little ship was so well made and detailed that the toy maker said it would bring great luck to the owner.

The father told his son the story and the boy named the ship Lucky because of it. And lucky He was in everything he wanted to achieve. But as he grew older the ship grew older as well and needed repairs. So the son went to the toy maker and asked him to replace the parts that needed replacing and it looked as good as did when he first received it as a boy.

The son then had a son and as result, he wanted to give Lucky to him as a present as his father did. The toy-maker was then asked to replace the old parts of wood on the outside and the inside as well as new sails and masts. As before the toy maker did as he requested replacing the old parts with new ones but keeping the old parts for himself.

Giving the New Lucky to his son and telling him the story his father told him, he was excited Lucky everywhere putting it under loss stress torture as a young boy does. Like his father, he received great luck but not as much and his father wondered why and figured its just because of the extreme wear and tear that his son had put upon it. Once more he took Lucky back to the toy-maker and when arrived he saw another new ship just like Lucky but instead there were the words Lucky inscribed on it.

The father was angry at the toy maker and said,
"When you built this boat you took some of the magic of my boat away. My boat is the original lucky not this boat!"
A person standing next time heard everything and asked.
"But is it really? you replace all the old parts with new parts and so those parts were used to make another lucky so is yours the original or is the toy makers?

哪個玩具？

有一位偉大的玩具製造商應他父親的要求為一個小男孩製造了一艘特殊的玩具船。這艘船製作精良，細節豐富，玩具製造商說它會給它的主人帶來好運。

父親把這個故事告訴了兒子，男孩給這艘船取名為"幸運"。幸運的是，他完成了他想要達到的一切。但隨著他變老，船也變老了，需要修理。於是兒子去玩具廠讓他更換需要更換的零件，看起來和小時候第一次收到時一樣。

兒子後來生了一個兒子，所以他想像父親一樣把幸運作為禮物送給他。然後，玩具製造商被要求更換外部和內部的舊木部件以及新的帆和桅杆。
和以前一樣，玩具製造商根據他的要求用新零件
更換舊零件，但保留舊零件。把他的新運氣給了
兒子，並告訴他父親告訴他的故事，他很興奮
Lucky 像一個小男孩一樣在失去壓力的
折磨中把它撒得滿地都是。和他父親一樣，他運
氣很好，但沒有那麼多，他父親想知道為什麼，
認為這只是因為他兒子的極度磨損。他又一次把
Luck 帶回玩具製造商那裡，當他到達時，他看
到了另一艘和 Luck 一樣的新船，但上面寫著
Luck 字樣。

父親對玩具製造商很生氣，說：

"你造這艘船的時候，帶走了我這艘船的一些魔
力，我的船是最初的幸運，而不是這艘船！"

旁邊站著的人聞言問道。

"可是真的是這樣嗎？你把舊的零件都換成新
的，所以這些零件是用來做另一個幸運物的，那
麼你的零件是原廠的還是玩具製造商的？

Two Gamblers

Luke and Larry are avid gamblers but there is just one issue they are very bad gamblers and lose a lot. One day Luke has a great idea that if they gamble against themselves they both cannot lose. it's impossible. So they flip a quarter and the winner gets a dollar.

Luke flips first and Larry says tails but its heads. Larry calls tails and the next time for 30 times and comes up heads every time. Larry thinks the coin is defective and changes his calls to heads but on the next toss, it's tails. This goes on for quite a while and Luke says.
"Gee, I've never seen such bad luck"! "The odds of that happening are impossible!" Larry says.
But what are the odds of that happening?

Infinite Buffet

There once was a buffet restaurant that touted to have as much you could eat for an infinity. For every plate, a person ate three more would appear. Of course, the customers came flocking because they always left full.

But the partner of the hotel decided he could make money without having a partner and decided to create a more than an infinite all-you-can-eat buffet. To do this he stated for every meal you ate two half meals would appear instead of three full meals which essentially meant six meals if it were to break down.

His partner takes him to court on the fact that there is no such thing as more than infinite anything.
Is he right?

無限量自助餐

曾經有一家自助餐廳，兜售所有你可以吃的東西。對於每個盤子，似乎一個人多吃三個。當然，顧客蜂擁而至，因為他們總是滿座。

但酒店的合作夥伴決定他可以在沒有合作夥伴的情況下賺錢，並決定創造一種不只是無限量的自助餐。要做到這一點，他說你每餐吃兩餐半而不是三餐，如果你想把它分解，這基本上意味著六餐。

他的搭檔將他告上法庭，理由是沒有什麼比無窮大。

他是對的嗎？

Two of you

If your brain was placed in another body, would that person be you or the body I left? Does the brain make the person or the body? What if your brain was put into a dog

or cat? Would that be you even though it is not a human body?

What if half of your brain was put into another body? Would that mean there would be two of you whole or two of you halved?

<u>Riddles</u>

I AM SEEN IN THE MIDDLE OF MARCH AND THE MIDDLE OF APRIL BUT NEVER IN MAY

or any other month from
night unto day
At the beginning of each
month, it is not seen and at
the end of each month it is not
seen but between the months
of January and December
it is never between

I CAN SNEAK UP IN FRONT OF YOU OR EVEN THE BACK WITHOUT YOU KNOWING, BUT ONCE YOU KNOW YOU'LL NEVER BE THE SAME

There are three doors. One contains life. One contains death and One contains purgatory. Each door has a guard that you can ask one question but not about the door he guards. One guard always lies, one guard always tells the truth and one guard repeats everything said.. How do you choose?

有三扇門。一個包含生命。一個包
含死亡，一個包含煉獄。

每扇門都有一個守衛，你可以問一個問
題，但不是他守衛的那扇門。一個守衛
總是說謊，一個守衛總是說真話，一個
守衛重複所說的一切。你如何選擇？

What is night but never day
Whats is round but not always around,
Sometimes light
Sometimes dark
Always wants with the waves to play ...

I can fill a room with just one heart or I can make the room dark with tears so that you will tear yourself all apart. Others may have me but I cannot be shared. Others may know of me sometimes sympathy is spared

I'M AS STRONG AS A ROCK,
RIGHT AS A CLOCK, I FIT
WITH YOU AS GOOD AS
ANY OLE SOCK BUT SAY
ONE WORD, AND I'M DEAD
AS A DOOR'S KNOCK

A LIAR SIGHS, A CRIER CRIES,
A DYER DRIES SO WHAT DOES
A LIAR DO WHEN HE DIES?

THE MORE YOU MAKE ME THE BIGGER I GROW, THE MORE YOU FILL ME, THE MORE YOU KNOW FROM SOMETHING I BECOME NOTHING BUT STILL SOMETHING TO SHOW.

I 'M ALWAYS AROUND TO WIN
ALWAYS BOUND TO FREEZE AND PIN
ALWAYS SOUND LIKE A WHIP TO CRACK
ALWAYS AROUND TO HELP YOU PACK
ALWAYS AROUND UNTIL THE RISE OF THE SUN
BUT I CAN'T STAY IN BRIGHT LIGHT, TO ME THAT IS NO FUN

TEAR MY BODY OFF, I DON'T
MIND
THEN SNATCH AND SCRATCH

MY HEAD, DON'T BE KIND
BE CAREFUL AND DON'T BE SHY
IF YOU TAKE TOO LONG FOR
YOUR FINGERS TO FRY
Shhh...shhh...WHAT WAS RED IS
NOW BLACK,
THROW MY BODY AWAY
AND DON'T LOOK BACK

The more you make of me,
the more you can rewind
the more you make of me the
more you leave behind

The more you make of
me disappears in the rain
and on the ground
The more you make of me
even without you around tells
me where you went with or
without ever making a sound

We are lost in the day
without a word to say
but once a night if lost we
can show you the way
We come at night and

ANTONIO KAZAN

you don't have to call

l
And if we get heavy make a wish
because we are about to fall

I have but a face and two of hand
but no arms and legs in which to stand

I will always be after you and never before
but you wish you knew more about me now and evermore

I am music that holds keys without locks
I am a source of the tune that is a part of an elephant in a box
The keys I have- unlock many doors
Once the music starts it does not rain- but pours

If I fall from the highest I fall divine
If I fall from the lowest, i fall fine
but if I fall in the water, i will fall in decline- paper

riddle me this? -what can
you touch be it a little or
be it much. But for it to be
nothing...nothing at all of it...
you will see it by shout or by call

You can see me and I could be you
You could see me and I could be nothing

You can see in me on a bright day and everything
But I don't get hot
And you see me in water you will be wet
but I will not

I can never ask a question
But I have a reply
I can never have a question
But an answer I could deny

I am wetter than rain
but feel no pain
I am as big as your hand
or as big as any land

I'm not fun when I'm new
But fat when I am
You can't eat me
but I need part of you
To make your life not blue

Throw me away when you need me
Bring me back when you do not
I can be on land
Or I can be on water
But you'll need me more
the further we are away from the shore

The more you have of me
the less you can see
The chore of having me
Means the more of light is a necessity

I am a word
that is not absurd
when I am headfirst
I am heavy
when I am backwards
I am not
Read me as one
not an abstract word

Three of me
the first has apple in mouth for a roast
The second wrapped in a blanket for the taste so most
The third by fire great with toast
See the three?

I have oceans and seas
but no liquid
I have a forest but no trees
Cities with no humanities
and lands with no fleshly- s
But not my fault
that's how I'm depicted

What am I?
If I am
what I am?
What am I?
If I am
I am
And that's all I am?
What I am

A man sentenced to death gets to choose
how he dies from three rooms.
The 1st is to burned at the stake
The 2nd is to be shot by firing squad
The 3rd is a pack wolves that haven't eaten in three years
Which room does he have best chance of survival?

What floats when it emotes?
What lies as it lives?
What drowns as it dies?

There is a one story white house. The walls are green, the floor is gray and everything else is blue. What color are the stairs?

I can't go left and I can't go right
If I have to many people it becomes very tight
I can go and I can go down
But I cant go outside
or out of any town

I once had two eyes round like pies
But now I have holes where everyone spies
I once could think
but now I'm just an empty shell
but heavy enough to still sink

I am said as one letter and written with two which is better.
Two letters there at my end
Two letters in the center to round a bend
A Single
A double
A single
is all i can say
But if you read me like this →
And if you read me like that   ←
I'm read the same either ....which way... → ←

The one makes me doesn't need me
but instead sells

The one who buys me doesn't need me
but instead expels
but the one that uses me
Never knows that he is
never hearing the last bells

I am alive without breathing as you do
But as cold as death moving faster if you try to pursue
I have armor but I'm no dragon
But I range in size from your hand to the size of
of a full steam wagon

You buy me to eat but you never eat me
My taste not my own but what give I comply happily
I have many a shape
and many a color
none of that matters
if my heart shatters
then nothing gets eaten
even if its sweeten
You buy me to eat but you never eat me ….

Using me once and you will smell like fine wine
Using me twice and I'll still be fine
Using me from my head to my toes
Keep using me though, and I disappear and nothing shows

I stare at you with my three eyes
Yet these eyes can't see
but you must follow me
Each eye not the same
each time they blink
gives you time to think
By only staring at my three eyes

You can hear me
but you cant see me
You can hear me
but you can't touch me
You can hear me
But without you
I cant be heard
What is the who?

When I'm mad
I turn red
When I 'm cold
I turn blue

When I 'm afraid
I turn white
When I die
I turn black

A man is trapped in a room with three doors, a table, bed, three chairs, a flashlight and knife on the table, and a sundial on the floor showing the time.
Behind one of the doors is a rabid dog that hasn't eaten in quite a while. Behind one of the doors, is a pit full of poisonous snakes, and behind another door is a glass room that magnifies the sun rays increasing the temperature to outrageous levels. How does he escape?

一個男人被困在一個房間裡，房間裡有三扇門、一張桌子、一張床、三把椅子，桌上有一個手電筒和一把刀，地板上有一個顯示時間的日晷。

其中一扇門後，是一條很久沒吃東西的瘋狗。一扇門後面是一個滿是毒蛇的坑，另一扇門後面是一個玻璃房間，可以放大太陽光線並將溫度升高到可怕的水平。他是怎麼逃出來的？

Drop, fop, hop, plop, pop, swap, bop, or top

Which word does not belong?

I can be alive
and grow and thrive
like you I need air to breathe
but no nose do I have or mouth to teethe
I hate water
because I cannot swim
but everywhere else I go
It will get pretty grim

I go round and round
but I don't get dizzy
I can go straight
or left or right
Wherever you take me
I won't put up a fight
If you break I do not bleed
or cry

but if you do not help me
you will be the one that will surely cry

You can't use me now
first you must break me
break me well
or feel my shell
break me nice
or you will have a mess twice

The child of a father
the child of a mother
the son of no brother
The child of no other
What am I?

I can hurt you without moving an inch
I can poison without touching
not even a pinch
I am the truth
I am the lie
I can live
or I can die
I am big
I am small
I can live forever
and make the greatest of things fall

Once given one
You may have two
Once given one
you may have zero

What am I?

What day is one day before the day
after three days after the day before Friday?

You may enter me but
Alas you cant come in
I have space
but alas nothing for you to put in
I have keys
but alas nothing to open
not even a lock if you please
I can remember what you do
but I have no brain

but for you I can be a great
head pain

How do you share 30
lemons with 25 people?

The Guru Says:

1st If the world is right a fool cannot make wrong, when the world is not right, a guru cannot make it right.

2nd Do not blame the entirety of wrongness on a simple thing. It is like tying down a man and expecting him to hunt for dinner. A man in a cage is the same as a dog in a cage. Neither is free to expound on their possibilities.

3rd The fool clings to Zen and loses his way on the road. The guru leaves the road on his way to find Zen.

4th To become a leader, you must find those who wish to win at what they do. Those who can win should be strong in something. Those who are strong can use the capabilities of others. To use the capabilities of others is to win their hearts and in doing so you master yourself. To master yourself you must be flexible as to say strong and weak.

5th When a bird has no resort, it will peck and claw; if a beast has no resort, it will chew and claw but when humans have no resort they be treacherous first before becoming animalistic.

6th The guru encourages good by what is good and discourages bad by what is bad. To reward one person and the world praises them, to punish one person and the world is in wonder of them. Therefore the best reward is not over-priced and the best punishment not overweening.

7th A great general asked the guru," Exactly what would make a government perish?"
The guru says," Winning every war every time."
"But why would that be a bad thing? "the general asked.
"Because to win every war may strengthen the government but not the people. To win every time may strengthen the people but also strengthen the ego of their superiors If the greatest of the egotistic ruler has a weak soldier then see if they win every war every time"

8th To read the books of the ancients is not as good as hearing to some, hearing the words is not the same as achieving the manner in which those words were spoken for some, to attain the words is something by which cannot be said so therefore a way that can be spoken is not the best way of Zen.

9th Jurisprudence and formula are but instruments of a government but they are not the government.

10th Governing is like tending to a plot of ground, get rid of the weeds and pests and you will be fine.

11th Those who have experienced Zen are changed on the outside and not the inside. Changing on the outside allows for a blending into earth-born society, the inside unchanging is the means staying as one. Therefore, they have a nonfluctuating inner life while on the outside adapting to external forces.

12th One who has never been burned by fire still knows not to touch it, One who has never been cut knows not to grab a knife. That being the case, the perceptive person can understand what has not yet occurred or what has occurred. By knowing this small portion then a total understanding is thus possible.

13th Duty is what is proper or obligated according to the rational. Courtesy is the controlling of one's elegance with a dash of feeling or not according to the rational.

14th Good food is the foundation for a good people. A good people is the foundation for a good country. A good country is the foundation for a good ruler.

15th Wood is not sold in a forest, Ice is not sold in the Arctic, and sand is not sold in the desert because the need is not there. So if there is plenty there is no desire, when desire is lacking, there is no strife.

16th Zen is strange and quiet, it has no appearance but appears, it has no model but it models. It's size is limitless and its dimensions are not calculable. Yet it is here for humans to decipher, though ordinary knowledge is not enough to grasp it.

17th Those who understand the Zen are not only focused on themselves but the world and beyond.

18th If you want to know the way of nature, watch he seasons, if you want to know the way of the shy watch the clouds and the stars. If you want to know the way of people, know what they want.

19th   If strength is up to the task, one doesn't consider it a hefty burden, when the ability fits the job, it is not consider difficult to do.

20th   The ways to evaluate people are: If of high status see who and what they promote. If they are affluent, see what they give, if they are poor, see what they refuse to accept. If they are envious, see what they will not take. Watch them change in difficulty and you see their courage. Show joy and happiness and see their self control. Hand them with goods and money and you can see their humanity. Show them fright and you can see their discipline.

21st One cannot drive a nail into nothingness. One cannot use a hammer in nothingness.

22nd A raccoon snare is there for the raccoon but once you catch the it you will forget about the snare, the same is said of words once the words get you what you want you forget about the words.

大師說：
第一，如果世界是對的，傻瓜不會犯錯；當世界不對時，上師也不會把它變成對的。
2 不要把錯誤的全部歸咎於一件簡單的事情。這就像綁住一個人，並期待他去尋找晚餐。籠子裡的人就像籠子裡的狗。兩者都不能自由地闡述他們的可能性。

3、傻子執著禪，在路上迷了路。上師在去尋找禪的路上離開了道路。

4、要成為領導者，你必須找到那些希望在他們所做的事情上獲勝的人。能贏的人應該在某事上很強。強大的人可以利用別人的能力。使用別人的能力就是贏得他們的心，這樣你就掌握了自己。要掌握自己，你必須靈活地說強和弱。

5、小鳥無計可施時，會啄爪；如果野獸沒有手段，它會咀嚼和抓爪，但當人類沒有手段時，他們首先會變得奸詐，然後才會變得動物化。

6 上師以善鼓勵善，以惡勸惡。獎賞一個人，世人稱頌；懲治一個人，世人都在驚嘆。所以最好的獎勵不是高估，最好的懲罰不是自負。

7 大將軍問上師："究竟什麼會使政府滅亡？"

大師說，"每次都贏得每一場戰爭。"

"但為什麼那會是一件壞事呢？"將軍問道。

"因為贏得每一場戰爭可能會加強政府而不是人

民。每次都贏，可以增強人民，也可以增強上級的自我

第八條　讀古書不如聽有人聽，聽話不等於達到有人說的話，得話是不能說的，所以可以說的方式不是禪的最佳方式。

第九條　法理和公式只是政府的工具，但它們不是政府。

十治好似耕田，除草除蟲，便萬事大吉。

11、體驗過禪的人，外在變，內在不變。外在變化可以融入土生社會，內在不變是保持一體的手段。因此，他們在外部適應外力的同時，擁有穩定的內在生活。

十二未曾被火燒過仍知不觸，未曾被割過知不抓刀。既然如此，有洞察力的人就可以理解尚未發生的事情或已經發生的事情。通過了解這一小部分，就有可能全面了解。

義務 13 是到期或基於原因的義務。禮貌是對一個人的優雅與否的控制。

第十四條　　食為好人之本。好人是好國家的基礎。一個好的國家是一個好的統治者的基礎。

15 森林不賣木頭，北極不賣冰，沙
漠不賣沙子，因為那裡沒有需求。
故多則無欲，欲少則無爭。
十六禪出奇地靜止，無形而在場，無形而有形。
它的大小是無限的，它的大小是不可計算的。然
而，人類可以在這裡破譯，雖然普通知識不足以
掌握它。
17 悟禪者，不只著眼於自己，更著眼於世間與
超越。
18、欲知天道，看四時；如果你想知道害羞的
方式，看星星。如果你想知道人們知道他們想要
什麼的方式。
19、不要認為做自己能做的事情是沉重的負
擔，不要認為自己的能力適合這份工作就很難做
到。

.

20、評價人的方法是：地位高，看他們在推銷誰，推銷什麼。如果他們富有，看看他們給予什麼，如果他們貧窮，看看他們拒絕什麼。如果他們嫉妒，看看他們不會接受什麼。觀察他們在難度上的變化，你會看到他們的勇氣。表現出喜悅和幸福，並看到他們的自製力。給他們物品和金錢，你就能看到他們的人性。

向他們展示恐懼，你就會看到他們的紀律。

21日不能把釘子釘入虛無。一個人不能在虛無中使用錘子。

22　　浣熊的網羅是為浣熊準備的，但一旦抓住它，你就忘記了網羅，一旦得到了你想要的，你就忘記了這個詞。